PUFFIN BOOKS

CINDY AND THE SILVER ENCHANTRESS

'Run away, Cindy,' cried the children. 'Run away before the Silver Enchantress catches you in her Magic Pool and changes you into . . . a fish!'

Cindy stared at them all, horror-struck.

'Run away,' they pleaded, 'before it is too late.'

Waking one night to find her room bathed in moonlight, Cindy heard a tinkling voice, faint and far off, enticing her to come out and dance amongst the silvery dewdrops. Little did she know that this was the voice of the moon, the Silver Enchantress whose terrible power was growing night by night. Bewitched, Cindy followed the silvery path that led the way between the midnight bushes towards the Enchantress's Magic Pool. Only the courage and daring of three other victims of the Enchantress's witchery saved Cindy from a fate as awful as theirs.

But the Enchantress was not to be cheated of her prey. On the following night, she took a terrible revenge . . . and caught little Benjie, Cindy's younger brother.

Cindy's desperate race against time to save Benjie from the vile clutches of the Silver Enchantress makes a mysterious and magical tale. It will keep readers of eight and over enthralled.

Cindy

and the
Silver Enchantress

Margaret Rogers

Illustrated by Riana Duncan

Puffin Books

Puffin Books, Penguin Books Ltd, Harmondsworth, Middlesex, England
Penguin Books, 625 Madison Avenue, New York, New York 10022, U.S.A.
Penguin Books Australia Ltd, Ringwood, Victoria, Australia
Penguin Books Canada Ltd, 2801 John Street, Markham, Ontario, Canada L3R 1B4
Penguin Books (N.Z.) Ltd, 182–190 Wairau Road, Auckland 10, New Zealand

—

First published by Andersen Press Limited 1978
Published in Puffin Books 1982

—

Copyright © Margaret Rogers, 1978
Illustrations copyright © Andersen Press Limited, 1978
All rights reserved

—

Printed and bound in Great Britain by
Cox & Wyman Ltd, Reading
Set in Linotron Sabon by
Rowland Phototypesetting Ltd
Bury St Edmunds, Suffolk

Chapter 1

The children crouched on the window seat, looking out at the moon. Cindy, who had dreamed her eight years away, gazed at it with shining eyes.

'It's magic,' she whispered. 'It's a silver enchantress.' (Enchantress was a new word they had discussed at school.)

'What's "chantress"?' asked Benjie, who didn't yet go to school to meet new words.

'It means a witch,' said Stuart, in a lordly way, for at ten he knew *everything*.

'That's what the moon is really. A witch, a white witch.'

'Witches are always dressed in black,' said Benjie. 'What's a white witch?'

Stuart sighed. The trouble with Benjie was, there was no end to his questions. 'A white witch uses her magic to do good.'

Cindy stirred at the window and smiled her secret smile. 'I still think she's a silver enchantress.'

Out in the garden, where the dark bushes bordered the silvery lawn, a little white rabbit gazed up at the children's window.

'I'm worried about them. The Silver Enchantress waxes stronger each minute, I can feel her power, seeking, searching, for a new victim.'

The long-legged hare beside her fixed his sad, brown eyes on Stuart's face. 'You needn't worry about the big boy. He's a disbeliever. Thinks he knows it all, all on his own.'

A jackdaw hopped nearer to them. 'You don't worry about the little boy either; him too young, too full of questions.'

'But the girl . . .'

They all gazed at Cindy's moon-rapt face. The white rabbit sighed.

'She's a moon-gazer – just ripe for the plucking.'

Back in the house, Father opened the bedroom door.

'Okay, okay,' he bellowed. 'Cut it out, kids. Back into bed, heads down, eyes shut, SLEEP!'

The children obeyed; and within minutes, Stuart and Benjie were sound asleep. Cindy could tell by their quiet, even breathing, and the little snorts Benjie gave as he sucked his thumb.

'It's all right now,' said the hare. 'They've gone to bed. Come away, White Rabbit.'

White Rabbit shook her silken ears. 'They've gone to bed, but who can say they've gone to sleep? See how the Silver Enchantress probes the glass, seeking, searching. She does not think the little girl sleeps.'

Cindy stirred in her bed. She sat up and gazed at the silver patterns the moonlight was drawing on the bedroom wall.

'I don't feel a bit sleepy,' she said to herself; and she tiptoed back to the window seat. There were patterns in the garden, too, a patchwork of silver and shade. And the moon was smiling brightly down at her. Faint and far-off, she heard a tinkling voice, like the music of glass bells.

'Come outside, Cindy. Come outside and join my patchwork pattern. Play on my silver paths. Come outside.'

Cindy shivered with excitement. Should she go? She looked at her sleeping brothers. What an adventure to tell them in the morning!

'Come outside, Cindy,' called the distant voice again, fragile and cool as ice. 'Come outside and dance in the dewdrops. Follow my silver paths. Come outside.'

Cindy looked out of the window again. 'I'm coming,'

she cried in her secret heart — but n[...]
hear her. She slipped her jeans on under [...]
her red woolly dressing gown over the [...]
slippers because the moonlight looked so c[...]
the tree.' Cautiously she opened the window a[...]
onto the ledge. 'I'm coming, I'm coming,' sang [...]
and the moon seemed to guide her feet down the b[...]
of the old plum tree.

'The Silver Enchantress has caught her,' sighed Brown
Hare.

'Not till she looks in the Magic Pool,' retorted White
Rabbit. 'We must distract her; get her out of the moonlight
for just one minute.'

'Me — I'll try first,' croaked Jackdaw.

He hobbled across the silver grass towards Cindy, playing lame — but her eyes were fixed on the shining moon,
and she saw nothing.

'Fly between her and the Silver Enchantress,' called
White Rabbit, but Cindy brushed the jackdaw aside like a
cobweb. She reached the edge of the lawn and stood,
uncertain.

'Follow my secret paths,' called the tinkling voice. 'See
where my silver finger beckons. Follow the silver thread.'

Cindy looked and there was a silver thread beckoning
her between the midnight bushes. She followed and it
broadened into a silver pathway through the tall trees of
the wood. White Rabbit hopped into the moonlight and
lay where Cindy's feet were bound to trip — but the ice-cold
finger of the Silver Enchantress guided her steps and no
matter where White Rabbit hopped or wove or jumped,
Cindy noticed nothing.

'It's no use, White Rabbit,' cried Brown Hare. 'The
Silver Enchantress will not let her see us.'

'If only we could stop the Silver Enchantress seeing,'
sighed White Rabbit.

'Impossible,' croaked Jackdaw. 'On a night as clear as
this, she can see everything.'

. r!' cried White Rabbit. 'There you have it. What
..eed is a cloud, to hide her face, for just *one* minute, so
we can open Cindy's eyes.'

'I will search on the mountainside,' said Brown Hare,
bounding through the trees.

'And me, I will try the fields, in case there's a mist rising,'
croaked Jackdaw.

'And I will watch and pray,' whispered White Rabbit.

Cindy glided silently along the magic path. Moon-rapt,
her eyes saw only the silver ribbon unwinding, leading her
on, on; her ears heard only the tinkling music of the moon,
promising strange sights, wonderful adventures.

'Help me, creatures of the forest,' cried White Rabbit.
'Help me slow her footsteps.'

'I will help,' called a spider, spinning his moon-spangled
web before her eyes.

Cindy stopped. 'How beautiful,' she breathed. 'A lace
cap, fit for a queen.' She reached out to touch it, but the icy
fingers of the Silver Enchantress crumpled it to nothing.

'Come along, Cindy,' called the bell-brittle voice. 'There
is no time to dally. Follow my silver pathway to its very
end.'

High on the mountainside, Brown Hare paused, searching the sky for clouds. There was just one, a baby puff,
frolicking round the mountain top. 'So small,' breathed
Brown Hare. 'Yet just half a minute might be long enough.'
And he called to the little cloud.

'Hide the moon's face?' she cried. 'Why, that would be a
great adventure! But am I big enough, do you think?'

'You won't know unless you try,' said Brown Hare.

'Then I'll try,' laughed the little cloud. 'Lead me to the
moon, Mr Hare.'

Cindy was nearing the end of the ribbon pathway.
Ahead, she could see it broadening to a stream, a river of
liquid silver.

'We must stop her,' cried White Rabbit, 'before she
looks into the pool.'

'We will try,' called the squirrels, seizing acorns from their store. They aimed – two, three, four, five sharp blows hit Cindy on the head.

'Ouch!' she wailed, stopping and staring up into the massive gloom of the oaks. It was black, impenetrable, up there. What strange creature was attacking her? Her stomach churned and her feet were rooted to the forest floor.

The Silver Enchantress gave a cry of rage, like the scrunch of ice crushed underfoot, and stabbed a lightning finger at the squirrels, toppling them from the branches. 'It's all right, Cindy,' she called, the bells honey-sweet again. 'I will not let anything harm you. Trust in me. Trust in me.'

And Cindy stepped forward to the banks of the silver stream.

'Follow me,' it gurgled and trilled. 'Follow me and learn my secret.'

'Hurry, little cloud, hurry,' panted Brown Hare. 'She has reached the magic river. Soon she will see the Magic Pool. You must hide the moon before Cindy looks in the Magic Pool.'

Jackdaw flapped past. 'No mist,' he croaked, 'but your cloud – it might just do. Me, I'll fly on to help White Rabbit.'

'Might just do,' snorted the puff of a cloud. 'Of course I'll do,' and she scurried all the harder, to prove it.

The silver stream broadened to a gushing river. Cindy walked its banks, mesmerized by its liquid, tumbling motion. Suddenly it cascaded over rocks and disappeared foaming into the Magic Pool.

'Ooh!' breathed Cindy. 'A lake of pure silver.'

'Lean over it, Cindy,' tinkled the Silver Enchantress. 'Lean over it and look – for you will see your fortune, written in the waters there.'

Cindy leaned slowly forward. She saw her hair gleaming in the silver waters – and even as she looked, the waters shivered and . . .

'Stop!' squawked Jackdaw. He dived over the pool and seized Cindy's hair in his beak, jerking it backwards.

At the same moment, the little cloud puffed in front of the moon and hung there, panting defiantly.

'Cindy,' called White Rabbit, Brown Hare, and Jackdaw urgently. 'Cindy, look at us.'

Cindy heard the voices and looked down. At her feet, she saw a little White Rabbit, with pleading eyes; a Brown Hare, breathing hard; and a Jackdaw, hopping up and down.

'Cindy, look at us,' they cried again – and as she looked, White Rabbit faded and the pleading eyes were those of a girl her own age. Brown Hare faded too, and in his place was a panting, laughing gipsy boy. And instead of Jackdaw there was a little black page boy in silver tunic and jewelled turban.

'Run away, Cindy,' they cried. 'Run away before the Silver Enchantress catches you in her Magic Pool, and changes you into . . . a fish.'

Cindy stared at them all, horror-struck.

'Run away,' they pleaded, 'before it is too late.'

Cindy turned and ran, back along the banks of the silver river.

'Hurry,' cried the little cloud. 'I cannot hide the moon much longer. She is freezing me away.'

'You must hide,' said the gipsy boy, running at her side. 'Quick, in here where the growth is thickest.'

He pushed a way through a tangle of blackberries into the heart of a hawthorn thicket.

'She will search but she will not find you here.'

With a splintering as of broken glass, the little cloud shattered into a myriad ice drops. One slipped through the branches of the hawthorn thicket and landed in Cindy's lap.

'Thank you, brave little cloud,' she whispered and dropped a tear of sorrow on it. Instantly, it fluffed out into a cotton-wool ball of cloud.

'Thank *you*, Cindy,' it whispered back. 'The tears of true sorrow shall always win over evil.'

Outside the thicket, the ice-cold searching fingers of the Silver Enchantress poked and pried – seeking under bushes, scouring the tree trunks, penetrating the thickest shades.

'I'm frightened, gip . . .' Cindy stopped and stared in horror. The gipsy boy was gone; Brown Hare sat in his place.

'Do not worry, Cindy,' said Brown Hare quietly. 'The Silver Enchantress's spell was broken only while her face was hidden. Now she shines again, we are her creatures once more.'

'If *I* had looked in the pool . . .' Cindy, hesitated, '. . . I would have changed into *something* too?'

Brown Hare nodded.

Cindy buried her head in her hands – and gave a shriek of horror! The Silver Enchantress's fingers probed through the blackberry tangle and Brown Hare dragged Cindy to the furthest depths of the thicket. They stared, dismayed, as the silver fingers lifted branches here, pried under leaves there. Satisfied at last that no one was within the thicket, the Silver Enchantress glided away to search elsewhere.

'B–but my hair!' gasped Cindy. 'It's slimy and scaly.'

'Yes,' nodded Brown Hare. 'She was going to turn you into a fish. Where you leant over the water to look in, the scales started growing.'

Cindy put a cautious hand up to her forehead again. Yes, they were scales, from just above her eyebrows reaching half across her head!

'I might as well be a fish,' she wailed. 'I can't go home like this!'

'Don't worry, Cindy,' said a new, softer voice.

She looked down. There were White Rabbit and Jack-daw.

'Because you only *started* changing, the spell will be broken when the sun rises. You will be yourself again.'

Cindy breathed a heartfelt sigh.

'Thank you, Jackdaw,' she whispered. 'Thank you for stopping me in time.'

She looked at them all. They were beaming with delight – yet, in the depths of their eyes lurked unfading sadness.

'Is there . . .' she hesitated. 'Is there no way *I* can help *you* regain your human forms?'

'No way,' croaked Jackdaw, shaking his head.

Brown Hare sighed and looked down at his paws.

'You see, Cindy,' said White Rabbit, 'the spell can only be broken if someone loves you enough to risk their own life for yours.'

'I was a gipsy boy,' said Brown Hare. 'One of many who ran wild on the moors a hundred years ago. No one saw where I went – or cared that I didn't return.'

'Me – I was a little black page boy,' croaked Jackdaw. 'Many years before that. I had to open carriage doors for milady, and fan her at the ball. When I disappeared, they growled crossly and bought another. It was a hard life and me – I would not go back there again; but when I see children now, black and white together playing, I could wish to be a boy again.'

'And you, White Rabbit?' asked Cindy.

'I was a little rich girl, in Edwardian days, with pots of money for a father, and a nursemaid to look after me. The night the Silver Enchantress stole me away, Father was on a business trip, and didn't return till too late.'

'Too late?' asked Cindy. 'Then . . .'

'Oh yes,' said White Rabbit, 'there is a time limit even to the work of true love. The captive must be rescued before the seventh night of the Silver Enchantress's maximum power.' She sighed. 'Father did not return until the seventh night and, though he was broken-hearted, it was too late to gather the cure.'

'I . . . I'm sorry,' murmured Cindy. It was all there was to say – yet how puny, how inadequate those words to express her true feelings.

'Don't worry, Cindy,' croaked Jackdaw. 'We have saved *you*. That is what matters.'

'See, the Silver Enchantress retires to her cave,' said Brown Hare. 'Now the sun will rise. We will escort you to the bottom of your garden.'

Soon they were standing in the dark bushes looking at Cindy's house. Slowly the sky lightened and a line of pink edged the horizon. Cindy put a hand cautiously to her forehead. The scales were dry and loose. She brushed at them impatiently and they fell withering to the ground. Beneath, her skin was soft and smooth, her hair silky, as before.

'Thank you all, so much,' she breathed, and planted a kiss on each forehead; then ran silently over the grass to the great plum tree. Reaching the sill, she turned and waved. White Rabbit, Brown Hare and Jackdaw saluted gravely, then vanished into the shadows beneath the bushes.

Cindy shut the window. 'What an adventure,' she said to herself. She looked at the tousled heads of her sleeping brothers. 'I'd tell you all about it — only you wouldn't believe *one* word.'

Chapter 2

Cindy woke late to find the sun streaming through the windows and Father anxious to be off.

'Breakfast's on the table, lazibones,' he said, giving her a quick hug. 'Mrs Gammidge will be along later to see you're all OK. 'Bye, now.'

Cindy sighed. Mrs Gammidge was plump and pleasant. She was a sort of daily housekeeper and she did her best — only it wasn't the same as having a mother.

Still . . . the sun was positively shimmering outside. It was a gorgeous day for . . . a picnic.

Mrs Gammidge packed sandwiches and lemonade into Stuart's rucksack.

'Now where are you off to and don't be late back,' she said, all in one breath. She often ran two things together like that.

'We'll follow the stream through the woods to the lake,' said Stuart. 'It will be cool among the trees.'

Cindy shivered. The lake . . . among the trees . . . Surely last night . . .

'Are you catching a chill, Cindy dear, you'd best wrap up,' said Mrs Gammidge.

Cindy gave her a quick hug. 'It was only a sort of looking-forward-in-excitement shiver. I've got a cardigan and we won't be late back. 'Bye.'

Mrs Gammidge watched them skipping across the back lawn. 'A looking-forward-in-excitement shiver, whatever next,' she murmured and shut the kitchen door behind her.

The sun beat down on the children's heads as they emerged from the coolness of the woods onto the banks of the stream. Benjie stooped to gather pebbles and threw them in a shower into the water. 'See them splash!' he cried. 'See them splash!'

Cindy smiled to herself. How golden and happy it looked in the sunshine, tumbling and splashing along. It cascaded over rocks and disappeared foaming into the little lake. Cindy laughed out loud. She knelt on the banks and leaned over the waters. She saw . . . her laughing reflection.

'What's so funny, Cindy?' asked Stuart, leaning over beside her.

'Oh, just a dream I had last night.'

Benjie knelt down beside them. 'What did you dream, Cindy?' he asked.

Cindy looked at them both. It was such an impossible dream, here with the sunshine golden on the water. She giggled. 'I dreamt . . .'

'Go on, Cindy,' shouted Benjie. 'Tell us.'

She giggled again. 'I d—dreamt I looked in the w—water and it turned my hair to f—fish's scales!'

Stuart snorted. 'Pshaw! It must have been all that cheese you scoffed for supper last night. Father said it would make you dream.' He reached out a wiry arm and pulled Benjie back, just in time. 'Good job I was watching you,' he said. 'We nearly had drowned duck for dinner!'

Benjie was unrepentant. 'What is for dinner?' he demanded. 'I'm hungry.'

Cindy pulled a plastic cloth out of the rucksack. 'Let's find out,' she said – and spread it right over the footprints of a rabbit, a hare and a jackdaw.

Long hot hours later, the children wearily climbed the stairs to bed. Stuart and Benjie perched for a moment on the window seat, staring as the moon rose above the trees.

'Why is it so big and bright tonight?' asked Benjie; but Cindy had snuggled straight under the bedclothes and was asleep before ever Father appeared.

Out in the Enchanted Wood, White Rabbit, Brown Hare and Jackdaw met on the banks of the pool.

'Did you see the children picnicking here today?' croaked Jackdaw. 'How they laughed and played!' He sighed wistfully.

'Yes,' cried White Rabbit. 'I heard them and I was glad because we saved Cindy last night.'

Brown Hare capered madly round the pool. 'We saved little Cindy, pretty little Cindy, saved little Cindy last night!' He stopped dancing and beckoned to the others. 'Come on, be happy; let's go play on the mountainside,' and he bounded away, with the others panting cheerfully behind.

So no one was watching as the Silver Enchantress glided along her secret paths, through the Enchanted Wood and across the lawn, to peer through the branches of the plum tree at the sleeping children.

'Last night I was robbed,' she whispered – and the words hung in icicles from the windowsill. 'Tonight I shall have my revenge.'

She slipped a magic carpet of moon-silver under Benjie's sleeping form. It raised him gently from the bed, and glided, with its snoring passenger, through the open window, across the lawn and along the secret paths of the Enchanted Wood. Wafting it along from behind, floated the ice-cold laughter of the Silver Enchantress. It tinkled across the grass and cracked a windowpane. Cindy stirred in her sleep, then snuggled deeper.

Outside, the carpet of moon-silver glided over the magic river, until it tipped sideways and toppled Benjie deep, deep into the Magic Pool.

On the slopes of the mountainside, White Rabbit shivered; Brown Hare pricked his ears; Jackdaw stopped in mid-croak. An ice-rending peal of laughter shook the air asunder. 'Revenge!' The word echoed and re-echoed round and about them. 'I have my revenge!' And the laughter, wild and long, broke on the rocks of the mountainside and resounded over the country, far and near.

It woke Cindy, who sat up with a start. Laughter! Heart-chilling laughter of the Silver Enchantress! But *she* was safe in bed. Then what? Who? She looked at the other beds. Stuart? He was snoring as usual. Benjie? Oh no! Where was Benjie? She pulled back the bedclothes desperately – but in her heart, she knew. The Silver Enchantress had taken her revenge.

Quickly, she flung on her jeans, the red dressing gown, slippers, and tumbled down the tree. On the mountainside, the creatures too leapt into action. Speeding their different ways, all four reached the Magic Pool together. They took one look at each other, then leant over its waters. There, in the chill depths, lay a fat, silver fish, fast asleep.

'Benjie,' sobbed Cindy. 'Oh Benjie.'

Far off, floating down from the skies, came the fragile voice of the Silver Enchantress. 'Yes,' it crowed, 'that's Benjie. Only now he's Silver Fish and he's mine. You will never get him back, little girl.' And her laughter fell brittle on their ears.

Cindy stared at the silver fish, sleeping there in the Magic Pool; and her tears were dried by the fierce heat of determination.

'She shan't get away with this; she shan't. White Rabbit, you said there was a way.'

'If you will risk your life for his, there is a way.'

'And risk it *now*,' said Brown Hare. 'Last night, when she tried to steal you, was the first night of her maximum power. Tonight is the second. There are but five nights left, if you are to rescue him before it is too late.'

'I *will* rescue him,' said Cindy fiercely. 'Tell me what I must do, so I can start at once.'

'You must gather the ingredients of a magic potion from far and dangerous places. You must mix them all together; and pour the brew over Benjie. We will help you all we can; but only you can actually gather the ingredients.'

'What are the ingredients?' asked Cindy.

'First, an icicle from the mouth of the silver Enchantress's cave,' said Brown Hare. 'I will guide you there.'

'Then, dew from the heart of a midnight rose,' croaked Jackdaw.

'Mixed with tears from a disbeliever's eyes,' said White Rabbit. 'The whole strained through a web woven from the hair of the Silver Enchantress herself.'

Cindy sat and thought. It was a daunting list, but collect them she would. 'Brown Hare will help me with the icicle,' she said, 'but where will I find a midnight rose?'

'I will go seek one out,' croaked Jackdaw, 'while you collect the icicle.' He flew off through the forest.

'The tears from a disbeliever's eyes is hard,' said White Rabbit.

'No, it isn't,' laughed Cindy. 'My brother Stuart is a disbeliever. Somehow, we'll make him cry. But how to weave a web from the hair of the Silver Enchantress?'

'I can weave,' said White Rabbit. 'When I was a little girl, it was an art we were taught.'

'Then I will gather hair from the Silver Enchantress when I bring the icicle,' said Cindy. Suddenly, she felt exhilarated. It all seemed so possible, so certain even. She had only to gather the ingredients . . . and Benjie was as good as rescued. 'Come, Brown Hare. Show me the way to the Silver Enchantress's cave.'

'Wait,' cried White Rabbit. 'First you must make your excuses at home, so your father will not miss Benjie or you. There must be no grown-up interference – no police, no searches – or all will be lost.'

Cindy stared. 'I'd forgotten Father and Mrs Gammidge. That's just what they would do if they thought we were missing – call the police and search the woods.'

'Have you nobody you could go and visit without them worrying?' asked Brown Hare. 'No friends? No relations?'

Cindy thought. 'Not friends; Father doesn't think Benjie and I are old enough yet to stay with friends. But –' her eyes gleamed – 'I know: Great-Aunt Sybil. We've stayed there

before. She showed us a fairy ring in her garden. But I'll need a letter from her, to show to Father, and that will take time.'

'There is no time to spare,' said Brown Hare.

'No time, but plenty of faith,' said White Rabbit. 'If we have enough faith, we can accomplish anything. Look at Silver Fish, Cindy, to make your faith grow strong.'

Cindy leant over the Magic Pool again and stared at Silver Fish. He opened one eye and stared back. She felt her heart quicken and faith stir strong in her breast. 'It's all right, Benjie,' she whispered. 'I'm going to rescue you.' She turned to White Rabbit. 'Aunt Sybil's letter is there on the mat.' And as she said it, she knew it was true.

'Go now,' said Brown Hare. 'Act your part well and I will meet you at the bottom of the garden when the shadow of the chimney reaches the last rose.'

Chapter 3

Cindy climbed in through the window just as Stuart stirred and stretched. He blinked at her in disbelief.

'Where've you been?'

'Just out in the garden, watching the dawn. You ought to try it sometime. I feel wide awake, alive – and it's only five o'clock.'

Stuart groaned. 'Only five o'clock!' He rolled over and in no time was snoring again.

'Good. That gives me plenty of time to pack and plan. Now what do I need? Something to cut the icicle – and somewhere to put it.' She crept about the house gathering a knife, and scissors, a flask and a jar.

Upstairs again, she packed them all into the nylon rucksack and started on a small suitcase, to make it look as if they were really going on holiday. She was just lifting clean pyjamas out of Benjie's drawer, when his Batman mask fell onto the floor.

Cindy drew her breath in sharply. She picked it up and pulled it over her fair hair. It fitted perfectly and what was more, even the eyeholes were darkened with a layer of black nylon.

'Bless you, Benjie,' she whispered. 'However would I have seen in the Silver Enchantress's cave without this?'

She slipped it into the rucksack and closed the suitcase. Now to dress. Something sensible for climbing mountains: teeshirt, jeans, and an anorak; it could be cold in the Silver Enchantress's cave. The thought made her shiver, so she tied her hair in bunches with her new scarlet ribbons, because scarlet was a brave colour. There, that felt better. Then she looked at her feet. She ought to wear shoes if she was hiking about all over the place; but Father might ask questions. Best stick to sandals. She buckled them on and was ready to face Father.

Cindy found him watching the toast and reading Great-Aunt Sybil's letter.

'Do you want to go and visit your Aunt Sybil? You and Benjie?' He frowned at the letter, and back at her. 'Funny, she hasn't asked Stuart as well.' Absentmindedly he turned the toast back over to the already-done side. Cindy rescued it with a laugh.

'We'd love to go. Aunt Sybil's fun. She believes in fairy rings and magic.'

Father looked up from buttering his toast. 'No wonder she hasn't asked Stuart.'

'When can we go? When can we go?' asked Cindy, dancing round him.

'The sooner the better, if you can't keep still,' growled Father. 'But what's Stuart going to do all day on his own?'

Cindy stopped prancing. She thought desperately. 'Couldn't he . . .?' Yes, that was it. 'Couldn't he have Desmond to stay?'

'His fat friend who looks like an owl? I suppose so. Might keep him out of mischief.' He looked at his watch. 'His parents should be up by now. I'll phone them and arrange it straightaway. You go and pack and then you can catch the half nine bus.'

Cindy danced up the stairs. So far so good. She looked at Stuart still snoring under the bedclothes. Impulsively, she wrote him a note.

'Gone to stay with Aunt Sybil. Back in . . .' She worked it out on her fingers. Five more nights of the Silver Enchantress's maximum power, plus the days in between the nights. She gave up and put 'a week' to be on the safe side. 'Enjoy playing with Desmond. Love Benjie and Cindy. P.S. Be good.'

She smiled to herself. That would make him snort. She propped the note on top of his heap of clothes.

'Cindy, Benjie,' called Father from the foot of the stairs. Cindy flew down them two at a time. He mustn't wake Stuart up, not yet.

'It's all arranged with Desmond's parents. Tell Mrs Gammidge he'll be here for elevenses and will stop the week. Now here's money for you, for the bus and for spending. Have a good time.' He hugged her briefly. 'Where's Benjie?'

'Just packing a few toys,' said Cindy guiltily.

'For playing with in between the fairies? Well, I can't wait for him. That phone call has made me late. Look after Benjie and don't be a nuisance to your aunt. 'Bye.'

''Bye,' called Cindy from the door. She looked at the sun. It was coming over the treetops, and she still had to see Mrs Gammidge. Oh why was it so difficult to get away, in the world of grown-ups? 'Come on, Mrs Gammidge, come on,' she muttered to herself.

And there was Mrs Gammidge, puffing in through the gate. 'Your father's late this morning aren't you up early?' she said, all in the one breath.

Quickly, Cindy explained all about visiting Great-Aunt Sybil and Desmond coming to stay. With a whirlwind hug and a kiss, she flew out of the door, leaving Mrs Gammidge standing bewildered by the kitchen table.

'Well I never did and did I see Benjie go too or not?'

She puffed upstairs, but there was only Stuart there, just coming to. 'Benjie must have gone with her, wake up young man.'

Breathlessly Cindy dived under the bushes at the bottom of the garden.

'You're late,' accused Brown Hare. 'The shadow passed the last rose half an hour ago. And what have you brought those for?' He pointed at the suitcase and the rucksack. 'We travel far so we must travel light.'

'If I didn't take them, Father or Stuart or Mrs Gammidge

26

would know we hadn't really gone. Can't we hide the suitcase in the hawthorn thicket?'

Brown Hare sighed. Every minute was precious – doubly precious as they were late beginning. 'And the rucksack?' he said.

'Necessary equipment,' retorted Cindy, diving into the hawthorn thicket. She flung the suitcase deep into it, narrowly missing White Rabbit.

'Sorry!' she called, and turned to go.

'Wait a minute,' cried White Rabbit. 'Take those ribbons off your hair.'

Cindy stopped in mid-flight. 'My ribbons? Why?'

'They might work loose and fall off up there on the mountainside.'

'But . . .'

Brown Hare stuck his head into the thicket. 'She's right, Cindy. If the Silver Enchantress found your ribbon in her cave, she could put a spell on you.'

'She could send you to sleep for a million years.'

'Just from a hair ribbon?' Cindy was scornful. In the bright light of day, this was an adventure. She didn't believe in sinister magic any more.

'From a hair ribbon,' said White Rabbit solemnly. 'She can put to sleep the part of your body the lost article comes from. The ribbon comes from your head . . .'

'And if she puts your head to sleep, the rest of you will sleep too.'

Brown Hare was getting impatient. He pulled the ribbons off Cindy's hair and dragged her roughly from the thicket. Her foot caught on a bramble but she jerked it free and set off after Brown Hare at a gallop, not noticing that the jerk had torn the buckle thread loose.

Brown Hare led the way through the Enchanted Wood at a steady lope and out onto the mountainside, with Cindy trotting doggedly in his wake.

'Now we must climb,' he said, and set off up the springy turf slopes at a pace that soon left Cindy panting behind.

The sun blistered down and the close-cropped paths were skiddy and steep. She paused for a moment to take off her anorak. Stuffing it into the rucksack, she gasped, 'Wait Brown Hare, wait. You're leaving me behind.'

Brown Hare turned with a sigh. 'You shouldn't have been late starting out,' he accused. 'And you'd travel faster without that thing.'

'It's got . . .' started Cindy; but Brown Hare had already turned and was loping upwards again. Grimly she set off in his wake. Above, the noonday sun scorched down, and soon her legs were aching and her feet sore. Her heart pounded as she struggled over rocks and up earth-loose slopes.

Brown Hare, impatient and on edge, chided her slowness.

'It's all right for you,' she muttered. 'Your four legs are used to mountaineering. My two are hot and tired and *empty*. And I didn't pack any food.' She finished on a wail of exhaustion.

'That's it,' cried Brown Hare. 'You need the fruit of the mountain milk plant. Wait here.' He bounded away, leaving Cindy sitting in puzzled stupor on the turf.

In a moment he was back carrying a stem of large milky-white berries. 'Eat these. Their juice is energy-giving. Eat fast, for we must beat the sun.'

Cindy ate, three, four, five. They were delicious. Milky sweet and refreshing. Six, seven. The effect was amazing. She sprang to her feet. She felt she could climb Everest, let alone a paltry magic mountain.

'Lead on,' she cried, and upward they strode together.

Gradually, almost imperceptibly at first, the air grew cooler. Cindy looked at the sun. It was drifting slowly down out of the sky.

'How much farther, Brown Hare?' she asked.

'Seven more ridges.' He too eyed the sun. 'Come, we must go faster. We must reach the rocks on the seventh

ridge before the Silver Enchantress rises, for there's no shelter here.'

It was true. The ridges were bleak and bare. If the Silver Enchantress rose while they were here, she would see them and all would be lost. Cindy ate the last milk berry, which she had been saving for emergencies, and forced herself faster, upwards, onwards.

Over the first ridge, and the frost lay sparkling and scrunchy on the ground.

Over the second ridge, and came the first sprinkling of snow.

Over the third, and it floated and flurried all around. Cindy shivered and pulled her anorak on again as she went, turning the collar up round her ears.

Over the fourth and the drifts lay deep and treacherous.

'Follow in my footsteps,' called Brown Hare, picking a way between them.

'My feet are frozen,' wailed Cindy. And they were, in sandals sodden with the clinging snow. It weighted them on her feet and dragged heavy on the loosened buckle.

'Think of Benjie,' said Brown Hare. 'For his sake you must go on.'

Cindy thought of Benjie – of Silver Fish, lying in the Magic Pool, and the chubby, mischievous boy he really was; and her determination grew strong again. It glowed inside her, so that though the fifth ridge revealed the slippery slopes of an ice-field, her toes grew warm again.

'Hurry,' called Brown Hare. 'Hurry. See, the dragons of the sunset flap their wings. Soon, the Silver Enchantress will wake.'

Slipping and sliding, skidding and skating, they gained the sixth ridge to see . . . the cracks and crevasses of a glacier between them and the rocks of the seventh ridge.

'No time to lose,' cried Brown Hare. 'The dragons of the sunset float away below the horizon. Hold fast to my ears and when I jump, you jump with me.'

Cindy seized the velvety ears and found herself soaring

effortlessly over crevasses. Ahead, the rocks of the seventh ridge turned black as the pink afterglow of the sunset faded, and then were ringed in silver, as the Enchantress stirred and stretched. Brown Hare pulled Cindy scrambling up the ice-slope and head over heels into the hollow beneath the rocks.

Just in time!

The Silver Enchantress slid gracefully out of her cave and lazily surveyed the world from her mountain eyrie.

'Now, how shall I spend this frost-crystal night?' she drawled. 'I know.' She laughed a silver bell-beautiful laugh. 'I shall go see how my Silver Fish likes his new pool.' She shook a flurry of snowflakes from her hair. 'To the Enchanted Wood.' And she sailed majestically away across the sky.

'Stay tight a while,' whispered Brown Hare. 'We must wait till she has gone out of earshot.'

'Out of earshot? Why? I'm not going to make a noise cutting the icicle.' Cindy slid the rucksack from her shoulders and took out a sharp knife.

'You don't need that yet,' whispered Brown Hare. 'If you cut the icicle first, the Silver Enchantress will know you are there.'

Cindy smiled ruefully. Of course. *She* should have realized that. 'But why not go inside the cave yet?'

'Look out between the rocks,' whispered Brown Hare, 'but carefully.'

Cindy squirmed forwards to where she could see out between the rocks. She saw the midnight mouth of the cave and the icicles fringing it like sabre teeth – and she saw two moonhounds, fiercely fanged, guarding the entrance.

'How will we get past them?' she gasped.

'I will draw them off,' said Brown Hare, 'but not till the Silver Enchantress is far away or she will hear the chase.'

'Draw them off . . . the chase . . .' faltered Cindy. She looked at them again, so tall and thin, with the legs of a greyhound and the fangs of a carnivore. Their eyes glowed fire-red out of cruel moon-pale faces.

'B—but they'll tear you to pieces, Brown Hare.' Tears rose in her throat, choking her on the thought.

'No they won't. I'm as fast as they and cleverer by far. Now listen. When I draw off the hounds, you creep into the cave and hide. Wait for the Silver Enchantress to return at dawn. When she sleeps, you must cut enough of her hair for the web. Hide again and when she goes out again tomorrow night . . .'

'But that will be two more nights of her maximum power gone,' whispered Cindy. 'One when she tried to trap me, one when she kidnapped Benjie, and two nights here — that makes *four* gone. Will there be enough left?'

'Three will suffice; one for the midnight rose, and one for the tears, and one to pour on the magic potion. Now, let me finish. When she goes out again tomorrow night, I will draw the hounds off again. *Then* cut your icicle and flee down the mountainside.'

'And you, Brown Hare?'

'I will follow as soon as I have lost the hounds.'

He turned and scanned the mountainside below. A silver glow bathed the Enchanted Wood. 'She will not hear now,' he murmured.

Cindy bent and kissed his silken ears.

'Good luck, brave Brown Hare,' she whispered.

'Good luck yourself,' he muttered gruffly.

Turning, he darted between the rocks and danced a Mad March dance right in front of the moonhounds. They rose to their fearful height, curled silver lips back from cruel fangs and leapt at Brown Hare. Cindy watched breathlessly as he zigged and zagged down crevasse-riddled slopes, now letting them clash their teeth only fractions from his heels, now leaping ahead in a wild luring chase.

Cindy took a deep breath and scuttled from the shelter of the rocks. Thank goodness the snow was frozen hard, so there would be no footprints. She slipped into the cave.

How dark it was inside! She stood uncertainly, staring into the gloom. Slowly, several bulky shapes materialized out of the darkness. She felt her way cautiously towards them.

The first rocked as she touched it and she drew back in alarm.

'Oh!' She let out a sigh of relief. 'It's only a rocking chair.' That was no good anyway. Once the Silver Enchantress came back, the cave would be filled with light, which would shine right through the chair.

She felt her way on towards the next shape. It was solid . . . and large . . . and had doors. She opened one. It was obviously a cupboard. Maybe she could hide in there. She stared at the shelves. Her eyes were growing accustomed to the gloom now and she could make out bottles of moonmilk and hunks of ice-cheese and packets of crater biscuits. So that was no good either. The Silver Enchantress would seek her supper there.

Cindy moved cautiously on to the third bulky shape. It was another cupboard. Hopefully, she opened the doors, but shelves of dried spiders and bats' wings, pots of snake jelly and frozen blood leered out at her. She shut the doors in a hurry. Then where?

Outside, the moonhounds came panting back. They sniffed and stared at the entrance. Cindy shrank back round the edge of the cupboard, away from the penetrating glow of their fire-red eyes. She slipped and fell through an opening in the wall of the cave. It was a very narrow passage, half hidden by the cupboard. She squeezed in and along until it opened into a tiny round chamber. There was just room for Cindy to curl up inside. She wrapped her anorak tight around her and twisted her feet beneath her, straining the buckle still further. But her thoughts were elsewhere and she noticed nothing. Nerves strained, she listened to the deep, panting growls of the guardian hounds.

'Oh Brown Hare,' she whispered to herself, 'I do hope you are safe.'

Chapter 4

The night dragged with tantalizing slowness for Cindy, curled in her frozen nook. The ice-cold of the cave walls penetrated her anorak and ate into her bones, but she dared not stretch or stir, for outside the moonhounds padded and prowled, sniffed and snuffled suspiciously.

Ice ages passed before she saw filigrees of silver dancing across the cave, faint at first, then whiter, stronger, until the whole cave was filled with dazzling moon-lightness. The Silver Enchantress had returned.

Cindy heard her laugh as she drank moon-milk and crunched ice-cheese in her frozen white teeth.

'Silver Fish is beautiful,' she sighed. 'Fat and lazy . . . and full of questions.' With a crackle of annoyance, the Silver Enchantress snapped a crater biscuit in her fingers. 'Why am I here? Why am I a fish?' She mimicked his voice in icy faithfulness and Cindy almost smiled. It was so like Benjie.

'Yes, Silver Fish is beautiful,' tinkled the voice again, 'but Cindy would have been better.'

Cindy's smile disappeared on the thought. 'Better indeed,' she scoffed to herself. 'Just you wait, you wicked Enchantress. You'll not have Benjie either soon.' She eased her cramped position and silently flexed her numbed muscles. And she waited till the Enchantress's breath rose silver and bell, silver and bell, in steady rhythm.

Then she crawled stiffly out of her hiding place, and opened her bag. What a good job she was still behind the cupboard; the moon-brightness in the cave was blinding. Mask first, or she'd never see what she was cutting. She slipped it over her head and adjusted the nylon-covered eyeholes. That was better. Now she could see without risking moon-blindness.

She peered round the edge of the cupboard. There was the Silver Enchantress, rocking gently in her chair, her silver hair flowing to the floor all around. Cindy turned to her bag and withdrew first scissors, then a nylon bag. Taking a deep breath to steady the jungle beat of her heart, she crept forward. Slowly she raised the scissors. 'What if she should wake? Or if the moonhounds should look in?' But even on the thought Brown Hare's words echoed in her mind.

'Think of Benjie . . . for his sake.'

Cindy raised her head and straightened her shoulders. For Benjie's sake, she'd cut off *all* the Silver Enchantress's hair!

Gently, with infinite care, Cindy eased the scissors under this strand, under that strand, snipping silently, and from so many separate places, one here, one there, that who could say if any were missing at all?

Once, the Silver Enchantress stirred in her sleep. She muttered 'Revenge' and shook her silken head. The strands caressed Cindy's hands like the kiss of snakes' tongues and she froze, an ice-maiden, save for the thump, thump, thump of her heart forcing its way up towards her throat. But, silver and bell, silver and bell, the Enchantress's breathing steadied again and Cindy slid her hands free of the silken tresses.

Under this strand, under that strand, snipping silently, steadily filling the nylon bag with numberless silver threads.

Once, the moonhounds growled and gnashed their teeth as they dreamt of an elusive hare leaping before them down the mountainside. Cindy shuddered and closed her eyes on the pictures of sabre-fangs, drooling warm red blood, that sprang before her. But, snuffle and grunt, snuffle and grunt, the moonhounds slept again; and Cindy snipped

36

silently on, under this strand, under that strand, cautiously, painstakingly, filling the nylon bag.

Once, she rocked on her feet, from sheer weariness, and the scissors slipped in her fingers. The bag slipped too, and four, five, six precious strands of silver were lost on the floor. Cindy took a deep breath and gritted her teeth. For Benjie's sake, for all their sakes, she must keep working, though her hand ached from the snip, snip, snipping.

Under this strand, under that strand, till at last the nylon bag was full. Her heart sighed with relief, but outwardly she dared make no noise. Cautiously, she crept behind the cupboard again. Close the nylon bag securely, keeping the silken treasure safe from view. Stow it deep in the rucksack, with the scissors and the mask. Oh how the moon-brightness dazzled her eyes! She fumbled to fasten the rucksack.

'Ah me!' The Silver Enchantress yawned and stretched. Cindy slithered and scrambled back into her hidey-hole.

'Ah me!' The Silver Enchantress slid gracefully to her feet and glided to the potions and lotions cupboard. The moon-rays gleamed and glistened their way even into the hollow where Cindy lay curled. She pushed herself back against the far wall, willing herself to disappear rather than be found. But the Silver Enchantress merely took a silver brush from a shelf.

She brushed her silken hair with snake-like fury, so the sparks flashed and danced round the cave, even into the nook where Cindy hid. One landed on her cheek and burnt it with icy fire. She nearly cried out with the pain, but bit hard on her knuckles instead.

'Now to go light the world,' breathed the Silver Enchantress and her laughter tinkled off the cave walls and crackled onto the floor. With a last flurry of sparks, she sailed out of the cave.

Inside, all was dark; but Cindy dared not move.

'Are you there, Brown Hare?' she whispered to herself. 'Be careful, oh do be careful.'

Suddenly the moonhounds bayed in fury and she knew Brown Hare was there, tantalizing, infuriating, drawing them away.

'Play safe, Brown Hare,' she whispered. 'We need you, Benjie and I.'

Now she must move again – and fast. She must cut her icicle and slither, slide and slip away down the mountainside, back to the Enchanted Wood, before the Silver Enchantress returned.

She scurried out of her hiding place and took the knife and the flask from her bag. Stumbling forwards through the gloom, she knocked against the rocking chair and sent it spinning round. Where had it been before? She put out a hand to straighten it, then pushed instead. It didn't matter, did it? Once the Silver Enchantress saw the icicle gone, she would know anyway.

Cindy stumbled on to the mouth of the cave. She stared at the fringe of sabre-teeth. Which one? Perhaps it didn't matter but she'd take a big one, just in case. Seizing it by the spike, she sawed off the largest of all, hanging right in the middle of the entrance.

'I really have burnt our boats now, Brown Hare,' she whispered, corking it into the flask. 'Now, run, and may faith guide my feet over those crevasses.'

Slipping and sliding, skidding and skiing, Cindy fled down the mountainside, her very speed loosening the buckle to its last thread. Far off, she could hear the baying of the moonhounds. They sounded confused, deep down, and echoing. She paused to listen.

'Brown Hare! Where are you?'

'Over here.'

It was a gasp rather than a shout. Cindy hurried to where it came from. There lay Brown Hare, panting, exhausted, an ominous red pool circling one leg.

'You're hurt,' cried Cindy, dropping on her knees beside him.

'A trifle,' panted Brown Hare. 'I let one of them get too

close and he nipped my heel. But I dropped them both down a crevasse for their pains.' The memory obviously pleased him. He almost smiled despite his leg; but Cindy wasn't listening.

'Nipped your heel indeed. I'd say he put his fangs right through it.'

She twisted her hanky into a tourniquet and bound it tightly round Brown Hare's leg. 'There, that will stop the bleeding.'

Brown Hare stood up on the other three. 'No time to lose,' he said.

'But you can't walk like that.'

'Of course I can. Just sometimes, it's a blessing to have *four* legs instead of only two.'

He hopped gamely down the mountainside, two feet and one, two feet and one, over the icefields, the snowdrifts, the ridges where snow floated and swirled round them. Two feet and one, two feet and one, Brown Hare limped gamely on, and Cindy was so intent on encouraging him along, she didn't feel the buckle slip away from the shoe, nor see it lie sparkling amid the frost of the first ridge.

Two feet and one, two feet and one, their progress was slower than safety. They were still on the grassy slopes above the wood when the Silver Enchantress stirred beside the Magic Pool.

'Hurry! Hurry!' It was Jackdaw, swooping low over their heads. Cindy grabbed Brown Hare round the middle and flew down the skiddy turf paths to the Enchanted Wood.

'In the nick of time,' croaked Jackdaw, pushing them headlong into the bushes, just as the Silver Enchantress swept past up the mountainside.

'Quick, to the hawthorn thicket . . . When she finds the icicle gone . . .'

'And her moonhounds down a crevasse,' chuckled Brown Hare.

'She will come searching.'

'Not today,' said White Rabbit. 'She cannot come while the sun is up.'

It was comforting but still they hurried until safe within the thicket.

'Here is the icicle,' said Cindy, 'in my flask. And here is the hair, White Rabbit, for you to weave.' She opened the nylon bag and the strands gleamed moon-bright within the thicket.

'She will see it shine,' gasped Cindy.

'Not if I build a hut of wattle . . .' interrupted a husky voice.

They turned and stared, dumbfounded. Brown Hare had vanished and kneeling in his place, a bandage tight round one thigh, was . . . a gipsy boy.

'You've changed back,' breathed Cindy.

'How?' squawked Jackdaw. 'Why?'

Gipsy Boy shrugged his shoulders, nonplussed. 'I do not know,' he said. 'We all understood it was impossible, without the potion.'

'That's right,' croaked Jackdaw. 'Potion within seven nights, or never change back again. Impossible.'

'But it's happened,' said Cindy. 'Brown Hare has become Gipsy Boy.'

White Rabbit spoke then, slowly, with dawning comprehension.

'I think I understand why. Because you were thinking of Benjie. Because you risked your life for him. That's why you've changed back. Oh Gipsy Boy, I'm so pleased for you.'

Gipsy Boy beamed. 'So am I,' he said. 'But that mustn't stop us helping Cindy save Benjie. Now, if I build a hut of wattle and plaster it with bog mud, the silver won't shine through. You start weaving, White Rabbit, and Cindy and I will build around you.'

'Not Cindy,' croaked Jackdaw. 'She must come with me to gather the dew from the heart of a midnight rose.'

'You have found one!' cried Cindy, delighted.

'I have found the *only* one,' croaked Jackdaw proudly. 'But we must hurry. Remember, you have been gone for two whole nights of the Silver Enchantress's maximum power. That makes *four* nights gone already. One, when she tried to steal you; two, when she took Benjie; three, hiding in her cave; and four, coming back down the mountainside. Tonight will be the *fifth* night. Come on.'

Cindy heaved an inward sigh of sheer bone-weariness; but she knew he was right. She stood up, and as she did so, the sandal slipped from her foot. She stared at it blankly.

'The buckle? Where?'

The others crowded round in dismay.

'You've lost it.'

'How could you?'

'Didn't you notice?'

'Where?'

Gipsy Boy spoke for them all. 'If you've lost it above the first ridge and *she* finds it . . .'

Cindy was frozen in horror. 'M—maybe I didn't,' she stammered; 'or m—maybe she won't.'

'She can't look for it till tonight,' said Jackdaw firmly, 'and then she may not find it. We must hope she doesn't. Meanwhile . . . we are wasting time. If we don't hurry, we shan't reach the midnight rose before the Silver Enchantress.'

Cindy drew a deep breath. Jackdaw was right. Worrying over the missing buckle wouldn't find it and they must get on with the next task.

'I'm ready,' she said. 'I will leave you the icicle flask, White Rabbit, for safe keeping.' She placed it where White Rabbit already sat, weaving, weaving, weaving the silver threads into a magic web.

'Good luck,' called Gipsy Boy, busying himself with his wattle walls.

'Lead on, Jackdaw,' cried Cindy.

'Not so,' he said. 'It is too far to go on foot. We must fly.'

Cindy stared in dismay.

'Think *small*,' croaked Jackdaw, 'and I will carry you.'

Think *small*! Cindy gazed at Jackdaw's back. That small? It seemed impossible . . . but . . . it worked! Either Jackdaw had grown or she really had shrunk, to the size of a . . .?

'Climb on my back,' ordered Jackdaw, and together they flew out of the hawthorn thicket.

Chapter 5

They flew past the Magic Pool and Cindy leaned low over Jackdaw's wing to look for Benjie. There he was, swimming in lazy unhappy circles.

'He starts to remember,' croaked Jackdaw. 'Bad time for him now; three, four nights, then he forgets he ever was a boy.'

'Why should he forget?' gasped Cindy.

'Because he's young, has so little to remember. Brown Hare, White Rabbit and me, all were older, all have more memories.'

'He mustn't forget,' cried Cindy. Looking back over her shoulder, she called, 'We *will* rescue you, Benjie. We *will*. We *will*.'

Far below in the dawn-grey pool, Silver Fish rose rippling to the surface to stare at the dark shapes of girl and jackdaw.

Suddenly, from far above in the moon-dark sky, came a piercing shriek of rage.

'The Silver Enchantress,' croaked Jackdaw. 'She has found the icicle cut.'

'And her moonhounds missing,' gasped Cindy.

One word wailed down the mountainside.

'Gone.'

There was a crackling, followed by a zinging, and an ice-spear plunged past them.

'She's breaking the other icicles off in her rage,' cried Cindy.

Jackdaw dived under a bush and they watched the icicles

flash white fire all around. One landed just beside their bush, nose embedded in soft earth, tail vibrating.

'If that had hit one of us . . .' Cindy gazed at it, horror-struck.

'Well, it didn't,' croaked practical Jackdaw, 'and she seems to have run out.'

It was true. All was silent and dawn-grey again.

'Whatever will she do if she catches us?' whispered Cindy.

'Climb on again,' ordered Jackdaw. 'If we fly fast enough, we won't ever have to find out.'

They flew out of the Enchanted Wood and past the Silver Enchantress's mountain.

High on the mountain top, out of their sight, the Silver Enchantress turned, rage spent, into her cave. She stared at the tumbled rocking chair. They had taken the icicle – they were gathering the ingredients of the magic potion . . .

She strode to the potions and lotions cupboard behind which Cindy had found her hidey-hole. On the top shelf lay a thick spell book. Impatiently she flicked the pages. Love potions; hate potions; icebergs, for the turning into . . . there it was: antidote to moon-enchantment. Her nail stabbed the ingredients in turn: icicle from the moon cave; dew of a midnight rose; tears from a disbeliever's eyes, mixed and strained through a web of moon-hair.

Moon-hair? They hadn't dared! Her eyes searched the cave floor for strands of hair, but her own brightness made spotting hairs impossible. How could she see? How tell?

Slowly she backed to the cave entrance. Yes, her brightness backed with her, leaving the rays to gleam into the cave. And there, where the rocking chair sprawled, four, five, six strands glistened on the floor. She darted forward and scrutinized their ends. Cut level, with a single stroke, not rooted as they would have been if brushed.

The Silver Enchantress ground her teeth. They had then *two* ingredients, and were no doubt even now speeding towards the third, while she was trapped here by that simpering heatball, the sun. If only something would happen to delay them.

Far below, over fields and villages, rivers and towns, Jackdaw's wings beat out an even, soothing rhythm; and Cindy basked in the sunshine, thinking lazy thoughts of Stuart and Desmond. She wondered what they'd constructed in the time she'd been away. Desmond was always constructing something. Last time it had been a tree house . . .

Her head nodded and drooped. She had travelled far the past two days and not slept the nights between. Jackdaw flapped steadily on and Cindy's head drooped lower.

Jackdaw was busy with his own thoughts. He was thinking of Brown Hare. 'Brown Hare helped Cindy get the icicle – now Brown Hare is Gipsy Boy again. Me – I'm helping Cindy. I'm helping her get dew from the midnight rose. Soon, I'll be Black Boy again.' And his heart sang within him.

On his back, Cindy was now fast asleep. Her fingers loosed their hold on the blue-black feathers; she slipped gently sideways, and tumbled slowly off his back. Over and over she tumbled, gracefully, slowly, growing larger all the time – for asleep, she was no longer thinking small – till she landed, her normal size, on top of a haycart.

She awoke with a start to see a pair of blank blue eyes staring at her from under a floppy straw hat. She looked around her, amazed, trying to collect her scattered wits. She seemed to be sprawled on a pile of hay, behind a tractor, and the blank blue eyes belonged to a boy about Stuart's age.

'An' where've you just dropped down from then?' he asked in a slow, country drawl.

Cindy blinked. 'You . . . you wouldn't believe it,' she faltered.

'Try me,' said the boy.

Jackdaw landed on the haycart beside her, croaking angrily.

'I–I fell off his back,' said Cindy.

The boy looked at Jackdaw, so small and black, and at Cindy, towering over him and guffawed with laughter.

Cindy seized his hat in her hands and pulled it hard over his eyes. 'Quick, Jackdaw,' she said, thinking small as hard as she could, and she scrambled onto his back.

Away they flew, leaving the farm boy gaping, as he lifted his hat and found himself alone on the haycart. He stared all round, then up into the sky, where he thought he saw the fast-diminishing shape of girl and jackdaw.

'Dad . . .' he began to the man driving the tractor; then thought better of it. 'No . . . better not tell Dad that. He thinks I'm daft enough already without tales of girls flying on jackdaws' backs.'

High up in the air, Jackdaw was croaking angrily.

'What do you mean by falling off my back? You might have broken every bone in your body. As it is, with having to stop to rescue you, you've made us late.'

'I'm s–sorry,' whispered Cindy. 'Will it matter?'

'Of course it will,' snapped Jackdaw. 'Now the Silver Enchantress will get there before us.'

He snapped his beak tight shut and flew like the Furies through the afternoon haze.

High in her lair on the mountaintop, the Silver Enchantress gazed out at the same afternoon haze.

'How slow that heatball simmers through the afternoon! Will he never sink to rest?'

Her thoughts turned to Cindy and her friends. If there were only a way to slow them down, put a spell on them. She snapped her fingers with sudden delight. That was it. A spell. All she needed was something of theirs – preferably something of Cindy's. Her eyes roved the dazzle of the cave; her fingers pried out every cranny; they found and explored the hidden nook where Cindy had curled; they traced the imprint of her warm girl's shape on the ice wall –

but hanky, or slide, or ribbon, or buckle found they none.

Outside, the moonhounds slunk, tails defeated, to the cave entrance, weary and afraid. The Silver Enchantress turned, furious, upon them, then paused, struck by a faint hope.

'There is nothing within the cave, but what might she not have lost hurrying down my mountainside?' She glared at the moonhounds. 'You have *one* chance to make up for last night's mistakes,' she snarled. 'Scour the mountainside, down to the lowest ridge, and find me something, *anything*, of hers. If not . . .' It was an icy whisper, and it chilled their moon-born marrow through and through. 'If not . . .'

She stared out at the sun as it slowly sank through the afternoon.

Far away, Cindy clung on for life itself, as the wind streamed her hair out behind.

'How much farther?' she gasped, as the golden ball turned orange.

'Too far,' croaked Jackdaw, angrily diving into the gloom of a pine forest. He whistled through the rigid ranks of the pines, standing blackly to attention in the sunset.

'Look behind you,' he croaked urgently. 'Tell me when you see her coming. There is not much shelter in a pine forest.'

Cindy craned backwards, watching the azure deepen to indigo. Far away the Silver Enchantress leapt from her cave with a cry of triumph. With incredible swiftness, the sky turned to silver in the east.

'She's coming,' Cindy cried. 'Coming like the wind.'

Jackdaw dived into thick bracken at the edge of a glade. He parted the fronds with his beak.

'See, the midnight rose,' he breathed.

Cindy stared. In the middle of the glade grew a solitary rose bush, with a single, black velvet rose opening for the night.

49

'How beautiful,' she murmured; but even as she spoke, the Silver Enchantress swooped over the trees and into the glade. She gazed at the rose, cold triumph creeping over her chiselled features.

'I'm in time,' she murmured, and bared ice-perfect teeth in a moon-cold smile. She plucked the rose with icy fingers. Cackling triumphantly, she shook it upside down over the bush.

Cindy stared dumbfounded as the precious dew dripped out. Slow tears trickled down her nose, even as the dew trickled from leaf to leaf. 'Oh why did I fall asleep?' she groaned to herself. 'We would have been in time.'

The Silver Enchantress laughed her bell-brittle laugh. 'I'll just make sure it is all gone.' She stripped the petals delicately, singly, from the rose, and scattered them like black velvet teardrops round the bush.

'Excellent,' she said. 'Now just a cage to make all safe.' She threw ice bars over and around the bush, imprisoning it safe within. 'That will foil their plans,' she gloated. 'I think I'll stay and watch awhile; and see them thwarted.'

Under the bracken, Cindy stared in dismal disbelief at the scattered petals. Her tears dripped unheeded onto the grass.

'Oh Benjie,' she cried inwardly, 'I've let you down.'

The Silver Enchantress stirred. 'It's boring waiting here. I wonder how Silver Fish is.'

Jackdaw whispered, 'Keep thinking of Benjie. She is sensitive to thoughts. If we can make her go away, we may yet save some of the dew.'

Cindy needed no bidding. Her thoughts were full of Benjie. She could see him swimming in sad, slow circles, forgetting he had ever been a boy; forgetting to ask his little boy questions; forgetting Stuart and Father and Mrs Gammidge; forgetting . . .

'Oh Benjie,' wept Cindy silently. 'Oh Benjie, what have I done?'

The Silver Enchantress stirred again. 'I can do no more

good here,' she murmured. 'The dew is gone. The bush is safe. I shall go visit my Silver Fish.' She rose on the thought and glided away over the treetops.

Jackdaw drew a deep breath. 'Now, dry those tears,' he commanded; 'there is no time to lose. She scattered the dew over the bush. We must collect it before it drips to waste on the ground.'

'Is there any left?' whispered Cindy.

'See, it shines on that leaf there,' said Jackdaw.

'And there, and there,' cried Cindy. 'But, Jackdaw, how do we get it? The cage . . .'

Jackdaw grinned. 'It's a cage meant to keep little girls out, not jackdaws. Think small again, and I will take us both in.'

No sooner said than done. Once inside, they both worked fast, tipping the leaves for the trickles of dew to drip into Cindy's jar.

'Oh Benjie,' thought Cindy. 'I do hope there's enough.'

'A boy again,' sang Jackdaw to himself. 'Soon I shall be Black Boy again.'

He tipped the last leaf over the jar. Cindy held it up to see how much they had collected. The precious dew barely covered the base of the jar.

'It's not very much,' sighed Cindy. 'If only there were another rose.'

Then she heard the whisper. 'Look under me.'

It seemed to come from the bush. 'Look under me.'

Wonderingly, Cindy lifted the lowest branches. There, in the heart of the bush, was a tiny bud.

'Ooh!' she breathed. 'So small. Is there really dew in that?'

'Of course,' said the tiny bud, in a prickly voice. 'We are born with dew at our hearts.'

Cindy hesitated. 'May I . . . Please, may I pick you?'

'You can try,' said the rosebud. 'If you want my dew for a good purpose, you will find me easy to pick; for a wicked purpose and I shall prick you and you will bleed to death!'

The tiny rosebud sounded quite pleased at the thought.

Cindy smiled at it. 'I want your dew for the best purpose in the world.' She picked it gently and placed it in the jar.

Suddenly Jackdaw gave a croak of alarm:

'Hurry! The Silver Enchantress returns.'

Sure enough, the sky over the pine forest was brightening rapidly. Cindy scrambled onto Jackdaw's back again, but he took off too fast; her foot was still dangling and it snapped a bar of the ice cage.

Jackdaw groaned. 'Now she will see someone has been here. What she will do . . .' He dived into the cover of the bracken.

Over the trees, the Silver Enchantress came stalking.

'Silver Fish is unhappy,' she crooned. 'He still remembers. But he is young. Soon, he will forget. He will forget all except me and my beauty.'

She stepped into the glade. 'And there you are, my precious midnight rose. Safe in your ice-cage. Those silly creatures – that little Cindy – they will not thwart the Silver Enchantress now.' Slowly, she circled the cage, gloating.

Cindy shut her eyes. She dared not look. Any moment now . . .

'Broken!' shrieked the Enchantress. 'An ice-bar broken! They have tried to steal the dew.' She laughed a brittle laugh. 'But they were too late – I had destroyed the rose.' She paused in thought, while under the bracken, Jackdaw and Cindy held their breath.

With a sudden movement, the Silver Enchantress smashed the ice cage into a myriad fragments.

'The bud!' she cried. 'When one rose dies, another grows in its place.'

She tore the bush apart, limb from limb, searching among the cruel thorns. There, in the very heart, she found the broken stalk where once the bud had grown.

'Gone!' she wailed. 'Gone! But they can't have travelled far with it. I will catch them.'

Drawing herself to her full, towering sky-height, she

poured the molten fury of her anger on the forest. The tinder dry needles carpeting the forest floor hissed and crackled and burst into flames.

'Cry, Cindy,' whispered the rosebud. 'Cry your hardest. The tears of true sorrow shall always win over evil.'

Cindy needed no bidding. She wept for Benjie, swimming his endless circles; she wept for Jackdaw and White Rabbit, still trapped by the Silver Enchantress; she wept for the pine forest, crackling and roaring in flames round their ears; and she wept for the midnight rose that would flower no more. And though the white-hot anger of the Silver Enchantress consumed the whole forest, the strength of Cindy's tears kept the patch of bracken cool and dry.

At last, the sun rose and the fire burnt itself out. Jackdaw and Cindy stumbled out of their bracken patch and stared at the charred black stumps around them. The pine forest was gone; and so was the bush of the midnight rose.

'Does that mean,' whispered Cindy, aghast at the thought, 'that no one else will ever be saved from the Silver Enchantress?'

'No,' said the tiny rosebud scornfully, 'of course not. It is a magic bush. See among the ashes where it shoots afresh.'

Cindy looked and before her eyes a tiny shoot poked through; and another, and another, with leaves opening and side shoots spreading.

'By tonight,' proclaimed the rosebud proudly, 'there will be another midnight rose in full bloom on the bush.'

Cindy breathed a sigh of relief.

'Think small and climb up,' ordered Jackdaw. 'We must fly back to the others. And don't fall off this time.'

Chapter 6

As the sun rose, the Silver Enchantress reluctantly retreated to her mountain top.

'Why are the nights so short?' she muttered. She stared up at her lair. There, in the entrance, stood the moonhounds, tails erect, ears pricked, evil fangs bared in red-rimmed grins.

The Silver Enchantress swooped on them. 'You've found something, my precious hounds. Where is it? *What* is it?'

She seized the silver buckle that gleamed between their feet. The moonhounds drooled icicles of pleasure. Long, weary hours they'd spent quartering the mountainside, ridge after ridge, sniffing, searching, to find it gleaming in the first grey of dawn on the lowest ridge.

The Silver Enchantress held it high in triumph. 'Now I can stop your progress, my meddling little Cindy. How will you walk to fetch your disbeliever's tears, when I have killed your foot?'

And she strode to her cupboard for the charms to mix her poisoned brew. She dropped them in a cauldron and placed the buckle on top. Then she boiled them with the white-hot fire of her magic breath.

(Below, on Jackdaw's back, Cindy felt her foot grow hot, but thought it just the heat of the sun, as it scorched down on them.)

The Silver Enchantress stared at the molten contents of her cauldron. 'It is good,' she murmured. 'The buckle is all gone.' Plucking an icicle from thin air, she stabbed it deep into the brew and ground it round and round.

(Below, on Jackdaw's back, Cindy felt the stabbing pain but thought it just her foot grown cramped and eased her weight about.

'Don't wriggle so,' snapped Jackdaw angrily. 'If you fall off, you'll lose that jar of dew.')

The Silver Enchantress laughed into her cauldron, where fragments of icicle floated in the brew. She laughed and tipped it onto the snow outside. There, it froze instantly, hard as death.

Below, on Jackdaw's back, Cindy's foot froze, instantly, cold as death. She felt it – and she knew. She tried to wriggle her toes – but inside she knew. The missing buckle was found, and all else was lost. Her heart sank within her, but she clung grimly to Jackdaw's neck, hoping against fierce hope that somehow she could cope.

All through the day they flew, and reached the hawthorn thicket just as the sun started to sink behind the Enchanted Wood. Jackdaw dived inside, tipping Cindy in a heap at Gipsy Boy's feet.

He pointed to a solid mud-packed hut in the deepest corner.

'Is that you, Cindy?' called White Rabbit from within. 'Have you the dew?'

'Yes,' said Cindy. 'We have it safe.' Cautiously, she tried to wriggle her frozen foot beneath her, but it would not move. 'How is it with you, White Rabbit? Does your web grow?'

'It grows,' answered White Rabbit. 'It was slow work at first, for my paws were clumsy. They were heavy on the strands of hair and broke them often. I nearly wept for frustration, as I thought of Benjie swimming out there in the pool, all alone. He needs my web, I thought, for how else can we strain the magic potion for his cure. I can't let him down, I thought. And as I thought of him, my paws turned back into hands and now my web is nearly done.'

Jackdaw listened to her tale and when he heard about her paws, he looked down at himself. The feathers on his

56

breast gleamed metallic in the fading light and his feet were still claws. He groaned and a tear trickled down his beak.

'What's the matter, Jackdaw?' called White Rabbit. 'You're not hurt?'

'No.' He groaned again. 'It's just that . . .' His croak faltered away. He was so disappointed.

'He hasn't changed back,' whispered Cindy, through the mud and wattle walls.

'He hasn't . . .' White Rabbit paused, thinking. 'Brown Hare risked his life for Benjie's sake . . . and he changed back into Gipsy Boy. I was worrying over Benjie and not being able to weave properly for him . . . and my paws changed back. Jackdaw . . . Jackdaw, why did you help Cindy get the dew of the midnight rose?'

Jackdaw stared at the walls. 'I did it so that *I* would turn into a boy again,' he said slowly. He drooped his head. 'It only works if you do it for someone else,' he muttered. 'And I was doing it for me. Oh dear!' and the tears dripped off his beak onto the ground.

Cindy picked him up and kissed the tears away. 'Don't cry, Jackdaw,' she said. 'You'll have another chance. I know it.'

'There is no time to cry anyway,' said Gipsy Boy. 'Cindy must fetch the tears from a disbeliever's eyes . . .'

Cindy groaned and stretched out her leg with the frozen foot, leaden and immovable.

'I don't think I can,' she muttered.

White Rabbit flew out of the hut; Jackdaw hopped near and Gipsy Boy sprang forward.

'Your foot!' he said.

Jackdaw pecked at it gently. 'Hard and heavy,' he croaked disconsolately.

White Rabbit felt it with soft girl's hands. 'Cold and stiff,' she wailed.

Cindy nodded, the tears welling in her eyes again.

'Girls!' scoffed Gipsy Boy. 'They only know how to cry.'

'But Cindy's tears are powerful,' said White Rabbit.

'Remember how they resurrected the cloud-fluff-ball.'

'Yes,' croaked Jackdaw, 'and they saved us from the forest fire.'

'Cry, Cindy,' they said together. 'Think of Benjie as you've never thought of him before. Cry, Cindy. Lean forward and cry over your frozen foot.'

Cindy leaned forward and wept. She wept for Benjie, trapped forever in the Enchanted Pool; she wept for Jackdaw, who would have no second chance if she failed now; she wept for White Rabbit, whose hands would only hinder in the animal world. Her tears flowed, warm and healing, thawing the ice and throbbing her foot to life again.

'Cry on,' urged White Rabbit. 'Cry till all is thawed, through and through.'

So Cindy wept. She wept for Stuart, who would never tease Benjie again; she wept for Father, whose Benjamin had vanished; and she wept for the pain as the blood pulsed through her foot again.

High on the mountain top, poised to sail the night, the Silver Enchantress stared in disbelief as a patch of ice before her cave melted and ran away, leaving a gleaming buckle in its place.

'Never!' she shrieked — and the echoes rocked the stars — 'Never in a million years! It is not possible to break *my* spells.'

She stooped to feel the buckle. It was a mirage, no doubt, imagination only. But her fingers closed on metal and the prick jabbed into them.

'Come,' she screeched to the moonhounds. 'Come! The spell is broken. There is nothing here to guard. She lacks but the tears from a disbeliever's eyes. If she gets those . . .'

And she swept down the mountainside, the moon-hounds baying at her heels.

Inside the thicket, they saw the bright light flood the woods and heard the hounds at large.

'What will they do to me?' gasped Cindy.

'Nothing,' soothed White Rabbit. 'But you must be wary. The Silver Enchantress will watch all the paths and the hounds will quarter the woods.'

'You would be safer off the ground,' croaked Jackdaw.

'On your back again?' asked Cindy.

'No,' said Gipsy Boy. 'Jackdaw would have to fly across glades, where the Silver Enchantress could spot you. Besides, you will need the strength of your full size to withstand her.'

'Then how?' asked Cindy.

'The tree walk,' said Gipsy Boy. 'The branches of these trees grow thick and close. Many a time I've scrambled to the edge and back and never put foot to floor. I'll lead the way.'

'And I'll distract those moonhounds from the scent,' croaked Jackdaw. 'With rustling twigs and shadows in the leaves, I'll keep them from your trail.'

White Rabbit turned back to the hut. 'I shall be quite safe within, finishing my web.'

Jackdaw flew off, croaking harshly to attract the moonhounds away. Cindy scrambled up a twisted oak after Gipsy Boy.

'If only Stuart could see me now,' she thought. 'Or Mrs Gammidge. "Girls wasn't meant to climb trees and do mind those jeans!"' She almost laughed out loud. She felt exhilarated; sure she could outwit the silly old moon. She shinned along a thick branch and swung across the gap between like a veritable monkey. That was it. She had broken the spell on her foot and she didn't believe in Silver Enchantresses any more. Her heart leapt for joy and she called out gaily to Gipsy Boy to help her jump the next gap.

Instantly, a shining silver sword plunged into the gap and fingers of moonlight felt along the branches. Instantly, the moonhounds plunged at the tree, snarling and leaping, baring sabre-fangs in the ice-bright light.

Cindy shrank back along the branch. She didn't believe in Silver Enchantresses, did she? Then how could she see

60

those prying fingers, how hear the gnashing of the moonhounds? Dumbly, she stared across the silvered space at Gipsy Boy. He pointed upwards, waggling two fingers at her earnestly.

Standing up cautiously, Cindy felt another branch, thick and firm, over her head. Silently she clambered up. Stood again. The next was thinner; would it stand her weight? Silently, she clambered up, then out along the limb. It bent and drooped sideways into a thicket of leaves. And there was Gipsy Boy, hauling her to safety, and frowning angrily as he did so. But he said nothing; just put his finger to his lips and led the way from tree to tree.

Below, the moonhounds leapt and bayed till the Silver Enchantress called them off and sent them again, searching, searching through the woods. They quartered this way, quartered that, with Jackdaw silently shadowing behind. Once they scented rabbit and plunged towards the thicket but Jackdaw rustled bushes in their ears and they turned away. Once they veered to where the trees thinned to lawns beyond, but Jackdaw croaked and whistled and, moon-brained, they turned away.

Gipsy Boy and Cindy came, too, to where the trees thinned out. Peering through the leaves, Cindy stared at the house. There was the plum tree and their bedroom window. How normal it looked. Father going to work each day; Mrs Gammidge cleaning and cooking; Stuart and Desmond . . . Desmond? Was he still there? Wearily, Cindy totted up days. No use. She had lost track of them. Days; nights. All she knew was tonight she must fetch Stuart, for tomorrow night was the deadline for rescuing Benjie.

Benjie! She stirred on the branch and stared again at the house. How normal; but how cold. Fierce moonlight bathed its walls. Everywhere she could feel the icy presence of the Silver Enchantress.

'You must go now,' said Gipsy Boy. 'There is no time to lose.'

'B—but the Silver Enchantress. She is g—guarding every-where.'

'If only you did not believe in her. Back there in the woods you didn't.'

'But I saw how she searched. And how the moonhounds leapt and snarled. I saw their sabre-fangs gleam silver. How can I not believe?'

'How can you *not go on?* Think of Benjie, Cindy. Of poor Silver Fish, doomed to swim in undying circles; never again to run on chubby legs; never again to annoy you with his questions.'

Cindy straightened up on the branch. She took a deep breath and swung down to the ground. Two paces through the bushes; she was at the edge of the lawn.

'I don't believe in you!' she shouted and sprinted across the silver lawn-lake.

'Don't you?' called the tinkling voice. 'Don't you really, Cindy?'

Cindy reached the lowest branches of the plum tree and started to climb.

'If you don't believe in me, how can you hear my voice?' The question was full of laughter; malicious, moon-cold laughter.

Cindy hesitated. It was enough. The Silver Enchantress's icy fingers whipped the next branch from beneath her feet and she toppled clumsily down onto the lawn. The crack-ling of the branches and Cindy's cry of pain as she crashed onto the frozen lawn woke Stuart.

He frowned. That had sounded like someone falling through the plum tree. Only no one *could* fall climbing that old tree. It was so easy . . . A thought struck him. Desmond might. He was clumsy enough for anything. Why, he'd only told Desmond about the tree that very morning, before he'd gone home. Groaning, he stumbled out of bed and over to the window. He fumbled with the catch, stuck his head out and gazed blearily down at the lawn.

It wasn't Desmond at all! It was Cindy!

'What are *you* doing there, Cindy? You're supposed to be . . .'

'Sssh!' called Cindy desperately. 'Don't wake Father.'

Stuart frowned again. 'Are you in trouble?'

She nodded. 'Put some clothes on and come down and help me.' She shivered violently as the Silver Enchantress directed freezing rays at her.

Stuart pulled jumper and trousers on over his pyjamas and clambered down the tree.

'Now, what is this all about? And where's Benjie?'

Cindy took a deep breath. 'Get me into the shelter of the woods first . . . out of the Silver Enchantress's sight. She's . . .'

'The who?' Stuart stared at her. 'Now don't start that nonsense again. That's only the moon up there.'

Far above, the Silver Enchantress snorted in rage and sent a flurry of hailstones onto their heads.

'Hail!' gasped Stuart. 'At this time of year. Better come inside.'

'Not yet,' urged Cindy desperately. 'We've got to rescue Benjie.' She struggled to her knees but was shaking so violently in the freezing moon-cold she could get no farther.

'Benjie?' said Stuart. Then he looked at his sister. 'Good God, you do look ill.'

'Just get me to the shelter of the trees,' Cindy cried through chattering teeth, 'and I'll explain.'

At last Stuart scooped her up and stumbled across the lawn to the trees. He dumped her at the foot of a large oak. Gipsy Boy leaned out of the branches.

'Up here,' he whispered urgently. 'Hurry.'

Wonderingly, Stuart pushed Cindy up to where Gipsy Boy could heave her on. Then he climbed up himself, not seeing or hearing the two moonhounds who leapt and gnashed below. Gipsy Boy watched entranced. 'He *is* a disbeliever,' he murmured to himself. 'Those moonhounds are figments of my imagination. Mine and Cindy's. They are not really there.' And he looked again at their drooling blood-red lips drawn back from pointed fangs.

'You are not really there,' he said aloud, and sure enough the moonhounds faded, ghost-like, into the trunk of the tree.

'Now what is this all about?' asked Stuart, loudly. 'And where is Benjie?'

Gipsy Boy shook himself free of his thoughts. 'Follow me and we will explain all.'

He turned along the big branch. Cindy followed in an icy daze, aware only that she had done her part, that Stuart was there, disbelieving, behind. And Stuart? He was wrapped in the thrill of a veritable tree route. Why had he never thought of it before? He'd climbed many of these trees but not seen them as a treetop road. What fun! Just wait till he showed Desmond this. Happily he climbed along, swinging across gaps, testing the strength of branches, almost laughing out loud at the wonder of it.

Suddenly, Gipsy Boy jumped to the ground.

'Hey!' cried Stuart. 'Aren't we going any farther?' Ahead, a stout branch curved invitingly onward.

'No,' called up Gipsy Boy. 'We have arrived. Help Cindy down to me.'

Stuart lowered Cindy off the branch, noticing again how pale she was, almost like a wax model and how cold were her hands. He jumped to the ground and squirmed after the others into the hawthorn thicket.

A little girl in a quaint old-fashioned dress ('like a picture out of Alice' thought Stuart) came forward to meet them. At her feet, hopped a dusty jackdaw. She gave him a grave nod, then looked at Cindy in horror.

'She is in moon-shock,' she whispered. 'Oh you cruel boy, how long did you keep her out in the Silver Enchantress's rays?'

Stuart stared at her blankly. Moon-shock? The Silver

Enchantress? It was all a nightmare. He pinched himself to see if he was awake, and it hurt.

'It does not matter, White Rabbit,' said Gipsy Boy. (Stuart's eyes grew rounder. He could see no white rabbit, anywhere.) 'I can cure moon-shock with a posset my old granny taught me. Meanwhile, here is our disbeliever. You can collect his tears.'

The little girl stood on tiptoe and stared into Stuart's eyes.

'Cry for me,' she commanded.

'C—cry for you?' stuttered Stuart. The gipsy boy, the little girl and the jackdaw all nodded solemnly. 'You must be joking,' he scoffed. 'Big boys of ten don't cry.'

'*You* must,' said the little girl. 'We need your tears.'

'I'll make him cry,' croaked Jackdaw. (Of course, Stuart only heard him crow; being a disbeliever, it never occurred to him that the croaks might have meaning.)

Jackdaw hopped near and pecked him hard on the leg.

'Ouch,' said Stuart. 'Call him off or . . . or I shall go straight home and fetch Father.'

Cindy stirred, where she sat, like a wax doll. 'No . . . no,' she said faintly. 'Not Father . . . not yet.'

Stuart knelt by her. 'What is this nonsense, Cindy? And where is Benjie?'

'That's it,' cried the little girl. 'I will show you Benjie. Then you will understand. Follow me.'

Wonderingly, Stuart did so, creeping through the under-growth as cautiously and as quietly as she. At last, she knelt down and parted the bushes.

'Look through and tell me what you see.'

Stuart looked.

'Why, it's only the pool in the woods.'

The little girl nodded in a satisfied way. He really was a disbeliever, seeing only the moonlight on the water and shadows on the bank. Whereas she . . . she drew back suddenly as a moonhound prowled past on icy pads, its fire-red eyes glowing in the dark.

'Where is Benjie then?' asked Stuart. 'He's not here.'

'Oh yes he is,' said the little girl. 'Go and look in the water.' She gave him a push in case he argued.

Slowly Stuart went to the edge of the pool and looked in. Reeds, some pondweed, and a fat silver fish swimming slowly in circles.

High in the sky, the Silver Enchantress hurled ice-darts at him but they shattered unnoticed on the wall of his disbelief. She gnashed her teeth in rage and ordered the moonhounds to tear him to pieces, but he turned back to the bushes, never noticing their clashing fangs. Impregnable, because you cannot be hurt by what you know does not exist, he crept into the bushes, and the Silver Enchantress wept impotently.

'I saw some reeds and pondweed and a fat silver fish,' said Stuart.

The little girl fixed him with Alice-blue eyes.

'The fat silver fish is your brother Benjie.'

He stared at her. The fat silver fish . . . Benjie? It was ridiculous. It was ludicrous. It was so ludicrous he had to laugh. A twitch, a choke, a guffaw, a bellow, and he was laughing fit to burst. He laughed and laughed till the tears flowed out of his eyes and he had to fish in his pocket for a hanky.

'Use mine.' The little girl handed him a dainty wisp of lace. She watched in deep satisfaction as he laughed and mopped and laughed and mopped some more, until the little hanky was wringing with his tears.

'Thank you,' she said and taking the hanky very carefully, as though it was precious, turned back the way they had come.

Stuart stopped laughing and stared after her.

'Hey, wait for me.'

They arrived at the thicket together. The little girl turned and stopped Stuart from entering.

'Go home,' she said. 'We have work to do here.'

'B—but Cindy?' he stammered. 'And Benjie? Where is Benjie?'

'Cindy is recovering already,' said the little girl, 'for Gipsy Boy is wise in Nature's remedies. Trust us, just one more night, and you shall have Cindy, and Benjie, back safe and well.'

'B—but . . .'

'Come back tomorrow night, after the moon has set. Now go home and be sure neither you, nor any grown-up come prying before then. Promise.'

She said it so urgently that Stuart found himself promising, though as he trudged away through the woods he couldn't help thinking it was all a bad dream and the sooner he woke up the better.

The little girl watched him go, then crept inside the thicket. All eyes turned on her, as she slipped inside – even Cindy's, for yes, Gipsy Boy's brew of steaming herbs was doing its work, and already there was a dawn flush to her cheeks and an inner glow back in her eyes.

'I've got them,' cried the little girl triumphantly. She held up the hanky. 'Now to mix the magic potion.'

'Wait till the Silver Enchantress withdraws,' croaked Jackdaw. 'Then we can mix in peace, while she broods out the day.'

So they watched and waited.

High in the sky, the Silver Enchantress saw Stuart stumbling homewards, tear trickles staining his cheeks, and her rage shattered the still of the night. In her fury, she tore chunks of ice from her mountain and hurled them down on the forest. The flashes from her eyes lit the landscape for miles around, toppling trees and knocking chimney pots flying. The gnashing of her teeth echoed from hilltop to hilltop waking the children. The blast of her outcryings ripped tiles from roofs and wires from pylons. 'Never was there such a wild storm,' declared all the parents.

Even Father awoke and wondered if he ought to phone Sybil, for he knew Cindy was scared of storms. 'Only the wires will probably be down,' he thought, 'and anyway, Sybil can cope. If I remember rightly, she used to enjoy storms when we were young. Thought there was magic in them, or some such nonsense.' He yawned. 'Maybe she can make Cindy believe that too.' He rolled over and was soon grunting gently again in sleep.

Deep in the Enchanted Wood, Jackdaw, Gipsy Boy, Cindy and the little girl crowded into the mud hut for greater protection and sat out the storm in silence. Only once did Cindy speak. She looked at the little girl in her quaint old-fashioned dress and said,

'What shall I call you now, White Rabbit?'

But the little girl shook her flaxen curls. 'No names,' she said, and she looked at Jackdaw. 'No names, until we are *all* ourselves again.'

Chapter 7

At last, the sun rose, banishing the Silver Enchantress back to her mountain lair.

Cindy, recovering more each minute thanks to Gipsy Boy's brew, opened her bag once more and drew out a fat little jug.

'We can mix the potion in here. First, the icicle from the mouth of *her* cave.' She opened the flask. The icicle slid, frozen still, into the jug and stood up in it like a baton. 'Then the dew from the heart of a midnight rose.' She unscrewed the jar and took out the rosebud.

'Tip me over the icicle,' cried the rosebud. 'My dew will melt it.'

Carefully Cindy tipped the rosebud so that the dew ran down the icicle, melting it all into the fat little jug. 'Now the tears from a disbeliever's eyes.' Cindy took the hanky. 'I told you Stuart was a disbeliever, didn't I?' She wrung the hanky over the jug.

'Strained through a web woven from the Silver Enchantress's hair.' The little girl opened the nylon bag and drew out a tracery of a web, that shot silver through the thicket as she opened it out.

'What will you strain it into?' asked Gipsy Boy.

Cindy stared. Her mouth dropped open. 'Oh,' she said, 'I was going to carry it in the jug. But I can't strain it into the jug when it's in it already!'

They looked at the other containers spread out on the ground.

'There's the jar,' said the little girl, doubtfully. 'But its neck is so narrow. Straining it through the web, it will spread out and we might lose some on the forest floor.'

'And the same goes for the flask,' said Gipsy Boy.

'I'll fly and find something,' croaked Jackdaw.

The minutes ticked like hours till he hopped back with an old enamel mug in his beak. It was chipped here and there, and for a handle, it had wire, strung through two holes.

Cindy stared at it in horror. 'It's a dirty old billy can,' she cried.

'Don't be so quick to scoff,' croaked Jackdaw. 'It's clean, 'cos I've washed it. It holds water, 'cos I've tested it. And what's more, *I* can carry it.'

Gipsy Boy held it up to his face.

'Jackdaw's right. There are no holes in it.'

'And he's washed it,' said the little girl. 'Come on, Cindy. You can't be finicky over containers now. What matters is that we mix the potion right.'

'Yes,' croaked Jackdaw. 'Mix it right and it won't make no difference to Benjie there that it comes from an old billy can and not your fat little jug.'

So they stretched the silver web, fine and delicate as gossamer, over the top of the billy can and cautiously strained the precious liquid through.

'Now we only have to pour it over Silver Fish,' breathed Cindy. 'Can we do it now?'

'No,' sighed Gipsy Boy. 'It has to be done in full moonlight, in the face of the Silver Enchantress.'

Cindy sat back with a groan. 'I suppose I knew that all the time, only I wouldn't acknowledge it.' She shuddered at the thought of having to brave that freezing fury again.

'You'll not make it,' cried the little girl. 'Once the Silver Enchantress has had you in moon-shock, the second time is child's play. Before you reach the water's edge, she would freeze you in a block of ice.'

'Don't worry,' croaked Jackdaw. 'Me – I've got it all worked out. Me and Silver Fish. He is busy down there now, practising jumping out of the water. Tonight, when you give the signal, Cindy, he will jump and I will pour the potion over him. That is why I brought the billy can.'

Cindy looked at him and at the enamel mug. 'So *you* could carry it easily,' she breathed. 'Oh Jackdaw,' and she kissed his soft black-feathered forehead.

Up at the house, Father woke Stuart, just before he left for work. 'What will you do all day on your own, Stuart?'

Stuart stared at him blearily: his mind was still a fog of half-seen figures; gipsy boys and old-fashioned girls, and surely a silver fish came into it somewhere?

Father was looking at him anxiously. 'Do you feel all right, young man? You're not sickening for something?' He put a heavy hand on Stuart's forehead.

Stuart struggled to his elbow. 'I'm all right, Father.' He winced for his head felt too heavy to hold upright. 'I'm just not properly awake yet.'

Father frowned. 'Mm . . . Are you sure it's only that? I could wait until Mrs Gammidge arrives, for once . . .' He sounded doubtful. Friday was a busy day at the office.

'No, it's all right, Father. I'll be OK.' Somehow Stuart felt it was important that Father left for work as usual. It had something to do with that old-fashioned girl – no telling grown-ups, she'd said.

'All right.' Father squeezed his hand gratefully. He was really lucky to have three such dependable children. 'You could ring your Aunt Sybil and see how Cindy and Benjie are,' he said from the doorway.

Stuart lay back and listened to Father's heavy tread clumping firmly down the stairs, the clash as the front door slammed, the boomf of the garden gate. Cindy and Benjie. And suddenly he remembered it all: Cindy shivering in the garden; the tree walk; the grave blue eyes of the little girl; how funny it had seemed when she said that fat silver fish was Benjie, and how important it was that no grown-up, or even himself, should go . . . prying? (That was what she had said, he was sure.) No one should go prying before the moon had set.

Downstairs, he heard Mrs Gammidge let herself into the kitchen. Thump! That was her bag going onto the table. Creak! That was the cupboard door where she hung her hat and coat. Ordinary, comfortable, everyday sounds. And yet ... and yet ... today they seemed far off and unreal. His dream, if that was what it was, seemed far more real than Mrs Gammidge wheezing up the stairs.

'You still lying in bed then, Master Lazibones, you should be up and about on a lovely morning like this.' Her presence in the doorway was solid, reassuring. Stuart watched her thankfully as she twitched back the curtains and let in a flood of morning sunlight. 'Come on downstairs, Master Lie-a-bed and I'll fix you a nice hot breakfast.'

For all his ten, independent years, Stuart felt oddly comforted. Just for a minute there, he'd really been wondering about last night.

Down in the hawthorn thicket, all was busy preparation. Jackdaw had taken command.

'It's time we left our hideout,' he croaked. 'We must all be safely hidden in the bushes by the pool, long before the sun sets. And I want Cindy and Benjie to practise their signal and I must practise my flyover.'

They gathered together all Cindy's equipment and stowed it neatly with the small suitcase, inside the wattle hut. 'I'll collect it all tomorrow,' she said, trying to be matter-of-fact, as though the night ahead were not the make-all or break-all of their futures.

She glanced round the prickly thicket where so much drama, so much scheming had taken place. It seemed almost cosy ... safe.

'Come along, come along.' Jackdaw was getting impatient. 'I know it's only midday, but we must all be part-perfect before that sun starts to set.'

High in the sky, brooding in her mountain lair, the Silver Enchantress was impatient too. Impatient, and afraid. Tonight, the last die would be cast. *They* had the potion. If they should pour it over Silver Fish . . . !

'But they won't!' The scream sent the moonhounds cringing on the ice outside. 'I shall guard that pool tonight, not winking, not blinking, and not one drop of that potion shall land on Silver Fish.'

Cindy and the little girl, Gipsy Boy and Jackdaw settled comfortably in the bushes by the Enchanted Pool. Benjie had practised his jump and Jackdaw his flyover, till their synchronization was perfect. Cindy knew when and where and what to signal, and there was nothing more to be done.

She sat and held the little girl's hand. It was so difficult, not knowing her name. Impulsively, she turned to her.

'Oh why won't you tell me your name?'

The little girl smiled. 'So that when the time of decision comes, you cannot pull me back, should I not want to stay. If you could call a name, it would be as a hook, a claw, to keep me here.'

Cindy sighed. 'You will go back then, after tonight . . .? Go back to your pots of money father?'

The little girl looked gravely at her. 'I do not know, Cindy. I try not to think about it. You see, if all goes well tonight, I shall *know* what I will do. But if we fail . . .'

'If we fail . . . you wouldn't . . .?' Cindy was aghast at the thought. She looked quickly at Gipsy Boy. He nodded his head.

'If we fail, then White Rabbit and I will be as we were when we saved you, Cindy. So you see, we build no hopes, make no dreams. But in our hearts we know the answer.'

'See,' croaked Jackdaw. 'The sun is setting in a ball of fire. To your places, everyone. And no more idle chat. All our thoughts must be of Benjie, and our rescue plan.'

Back at the house, Father turned in at the gate. Dazzled by the blaze of the sunset, he didn't at once recognize Aunt Sybil, standing on the doorstep.

'Hallo,' she trilled, beaming happily. 'I was just on my way home from a shopping expedition.' She pointed vaguely at an array of parcels and packages littered haphazardly on the doorstep. 'And I thought I'd call in for the night and take the children home with me in the morning. It's time they came to stay with me.'

Father's jaw dropped – so did his briefcase, with a clatter, amid the parcels. 'B–but,' he began, 'Cindy . . . Benjie . . . they've been staying with you for the last week . . .' His voice trailed off as he saw Great-Aunt Sybil's eyes widen in surprise. '. . . Haven't they?'

She shook her head at him in puzzlement.

'Then where . . .?' He opened the door of the house. 'Stuart!' he bellowed, pushing Aunt Sybil roughly into the house before him. 'Stuart!'

Stuart came running down the stairs.

'Where are Cindy and Benjie?'

'Why, they're staying with . . .' He clapped his hand to his mouth. Great-Aunt Sybil was standing there, shaking her head dumbly at him. Suddenly he remembered last night's dream. He sat down heavily on the fifth stair. Supposing it wasn't a dream?

He felt a gentle hand on his elbow. It was Great-Aunt Sybil. 'Come into the front room, dear,' she was saying softly. 'We must pool our ideas, and our knowledge, and see what we have to go on.' She steered him firmly to the settee. Father was pouring himself a stiff whisky.

'No you don't, George dear. We shall need all our wits about us. Now, settle yourself in your big armchair and light your pipe and tell me all about it.'

Only *all* didn't take long to tell. Cindy had left five, or was it six days ago, to stay with Great-Aunt Sybil at her invitation.

74

'At my invitation? Nonsense,' trilled Aunt Sybil. 'I wrote no invitation.'

'Well, it was *your* writing,' said Father. 'Cindy couldn't have forged it.'

That was true, thought Stuart. Great-Aunt Sybil's writing was like a delicate old-fashioned spider, wriggling across the page in frills and curlicues.

Father was fishing in his pocket. 'Here you are: see for yourself.' He passed the letter over with a flourish.

Aunt Sybil examined it carefully – first under the electric light – 'No, no, I need a candle!'

Father stared at her in disbelief. 'Sybil, my children are missing. Cindy . . . Benjie . . . and you demand candles!'

Great-Aunt Sybil ignored him. 'Stuart, a candle at the double.'

He ran to the kitchen, catching her sense of urgency, and soon they had a candle casting a flickering light on the table. Aunt Sybil brought the letter slowly down right over the flame. Stuart started forward. 'You'll burn it!' But the letter went right down through the flame and up again without even scorching.

'As I thought,' murmured Great-Aunt Sybil. 'There's magic afoot here somewhere.'

Father groaned. He heaved himself out of his chair. Magic indeed. And with Cindy and Benjie missing. 'I'm going to call the police.'

'No, Father.' Stuart clapped his hand to his mouth again.

'Why not, young man?' It was Father leaning, glowering, over him. 'Do you know more than you've been telling?'

'Sit down, George,' said Great-Aunt Sybil briskly. 'If the lad has a story to tell, he'll tell it better without you breathing over him. Come on, boy, out with it.'

So Stuart, hesitatingly, told the story of the night before. As he finished, Father rose in wrath over him.

'Why didn't you . . . ?'

But Great-Aunt Sybil was there again. She fluttered a hand at Father. 'Do sit down, George, there's a dear. I can't think with you towering over me.'

Father subsided into the armchair again and set about relighting his pipe to soothe his nerves.

'Now this is really most interesting,' trilled Aunt Sybil. 'Cindy called the moon the "Silver Enchantress". Now that was the name she had back in the days when *everyone* believed in magic.' She gave Father a reproving look. 'The story goes that for three weeks she was just the moon in the sky, but for the fourth week, when her light was at its brightest, she came to life, as the Silver Enchantress. Then you must beware and not go out unprotected in her icy light, or she might seize you and turn you into one of her creatures.'

'Is that what you think has happened to Cindy?' asked Stuart.

'No, no, not to Cindy, silly. You saw her yourself last night. But to Benjie, maybe. What did the little girl tell you was Benjie?'

'A fat silver fish, swimming in the pool in the woods.'

'A fat . . .' Father started up, but Aunt Sybil waved him down.

'Yes, that's possible. Pools were always enchanted places at night, especially with the moon silvering their waters. Now, what exactly did that little girl in the old-fashioned dress say? Think hard. You must get it right.'

Stuart concentrated. If he shut his eyes . . . Yes, he could see her face – flaxen curls and big, serious blue eyes. 'She said . . . "Just one more night and you shall have Cindy and Benjie back, safe and well."'

'Just one more night . . . Yes, that figures. The Silver Enchantress has only one week of full power, the three or four days on either side of the full moon. Well, full moon was three nights ago, so tonight is the last night of the Silver Enchantress's maximum power. It's tonight they must break the spell. Tonight is do or die.'

It was an unfortunate choice of word. Father leapt out of his chair and lunged for the telephone. 'Do or die!' he shouted. 'Do or die! We are sitting here doing nothing except talk a load of . . . of moonshine . . . while my Cindy and my Benjie are dead or dying out there in the woods.' He lifted the receiver. 'I'm phoning the police.'

'No, Father.' Stuart was there, pushing the receiver back down. 'Not till morning. There must be no grown-up interference till after the moon has set.'

'The boy's right,' said Great-Aunt Sybil firmly. 'If we call the police now, or even go ourselves, we shall likely ruin everything. Now I'll brew a good strong pot of tea, and you shall smoke your pipe, and we will watch for the moon to set. See how big and bright it rises. Unusually so for the *seventh* night of maximum power.'

Deep in the bushes beside the Enchanted Pool, the children huddled close together as the Silver Enchantress swept over the trees. She had stood at her cave entrance chafing for the last crimson glow to fade into night, then flung herself straight for the pool in the woods. And there she hung, cold and gloating, staring down at Silver Fish.

'You are mine, mine,' she exulted, 'and no one, NO ONE,' the word rose on a crescendo and fell spluttering into the water, 'no one shall take you from me.'

'When will you do it?' whispered Cindy fearfully to Jackdaw. The Silver Enchantress was so alert, so all-seeing, success seemed impossible.

'When she begins to think it's too late,' he murmured.

So they sat and waited, tense and cold. And the Silver Enchantress waited and watched, her eyes never leaving the Magic Pool.

Back in the house, Father growled, 'That moon doesn't seem to be moving at all.'

'No, George dear,' trilled Great-Aunt Sybil. 'It's been hanging over the woods all night.'

77

In the bushes Cindy stirred and looked a question at Jackdaw.

Above, the Silver Enchantress yawned and stretched. 'They haven't dared,' she sighed. The words trickled in an icy rivulet through the night air.

'Now,' Jackdaw croaked – and everything happened at once.

'Benjie,' cried Cindy, giving him the signal. Silver Fish jumped high out of the Magic Pool.

Jackdaw flew straight as an arrow across the waters, billy can swaying in his beak.

The Silver Enchantress, with a cry of rage, hurled herself at Jackdaw. She crushed him in her icy grip and the magic potion flew out of the billy can.

It flew up over the Silver Enchantress and smashed her into a myriad fragments of ice. It flew down over Jackdaw and Silver Fish, into the waters of the Magic Pool. They sizzled and hissed and dried up, and there sitting on the pond bed were Benjie, and the little Black Boy, complete with his turban and silken tunic.

Gipsy Boy, the little girl, and Cindy stumbled out of the bushes and danced round the two boys.

'We're boys again,' cried Benjie and Black Boy.

'And we've killed the Silver Enchantress,' laughed Cindy.

And they fell together in a laughing, tumbling circle.

Back at the house, Father stood up abruptly. 'The moon's gone out,' he said.

And so it had.

'Snuffed like a candle,' mused Great-Aunt Sybil. 'Ah well. I expect that counts as setting.' She turned to Father and Stuart. 'I think we could go to the woods now.'

The children in the woods stopped laughing suddenly. The little girl stood up, listening. 'Grown-ups are coming,' she said urgently. 'We must decide now what we want to do, or we shall be trapped here forever.'

Gipsy Boy stood up too. 'I know what I want,' he said,

I want my freedom to run and play on the moors; to live as *I* please, not be sent to school every day. I'm going back.'

He looked at the little girl in the old-fashioned dress.

'Yes,' she said. 'I shall go back too. While I was there, I never knew my father loved me, but he was so broken-hearted when I left, I must go back to comfort him.'

Cindy nodded sadly, and turned to the black boy.

'And you, Tembo?' She stopped in surprise. How did she know his name?

Tembo grinned at her, the white teeth splitting his face from ear to ear.

'No, I shall stay here. Before, it was always "do this", "yes, m'lord", "do that", "yes, m'lady". Now I can be a person in my own right. I can talk to you as your equal; I can share all your privileges; and I can be your friend.'

And so it was that when Father stalked into the clearing, with Great-Aunt Sybil and Stuart following breathlessly behind, he was met by Cindy, and Benjie, and Tembo – but Gipsy Boy and the little girl had vanished back through the mists of time.

'Whatever has been going on?' muttered Stuart to Cindy, as they trailed back home again.

'You wouldn't believe me if I told you,' said Cindy and smiled her secret smile.